GOODNIGHT GOON

A PETRIFYING PARODY

Michael Rex

SCHOLASTIC INC.
New York Toronto London Auckland
Sydney Mexico City New Delhi Hong Kong

In the cold gray tomb
There was a gravestone
And a black lagoon
And a picture of—

Martians taking over the moon

And there were three little mummies rubbing their tummies

And two hairy claws
And a set of jaws

And a loud screechy bat
And a black hat

And a skull and a shoe and a pot full of goo

And a hairy old werewolf who was hollering "Boo"

Goodnight tomb

Goodnight goon

Goodnight Martians taking over the moon

Goodnight bones
And the black lagoon

Goodnight mummies
Goodnight tummies

Goodnight claws

And goodnight jaws

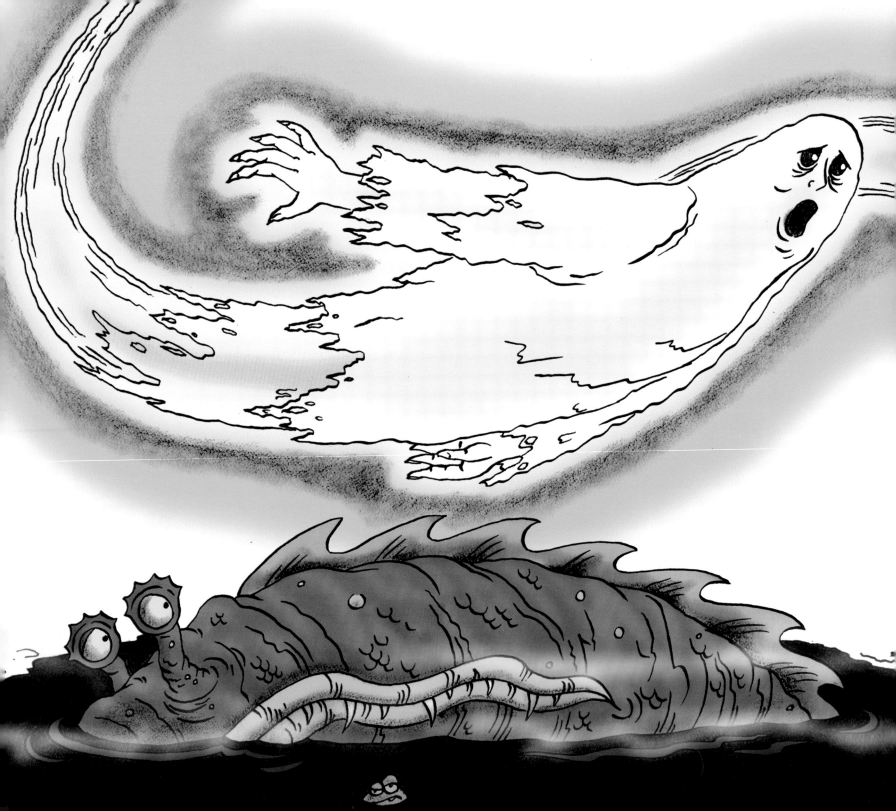

Goodnight moans
And goodnight groans

Goodnight screechy bat

And goodnight hat

Goodnight skull

And goodnight shoe

Goodnight creature

Goodnight goo

And goodnight to the old werewolf
hollering "Boo"

Goodnight you

Get under there

Goodnight monsters everywhere

Just for Gavin

ISBN-13: 978-0-545-20704-1
ISBN-10: 0-545-20704-5

Copyright © 2008 by Michael Rex.
All rights reserved. Published by Scholastic Inc., 557 Broadway, New York, NY 10012, by arrangement with G. P. Putnam's Sons, a division of Penguin Young Readers Group, a member of Penguin Group (USA) Inc. SCHOLASTIC and associated logos are trademarks and/or registered trademarks of Scholastic Inc.

12 11 10 9 8 7 6 5 4 3 2 1   9 10 11 12 13 14/0

Printed in the U.S.A.   40

First Scholastic printing, October 2009

Design by Marikka Tamura
Text set in OPTI Malou
The artist used pencil drawings colored in Photoshop to create the illustrations for this book.